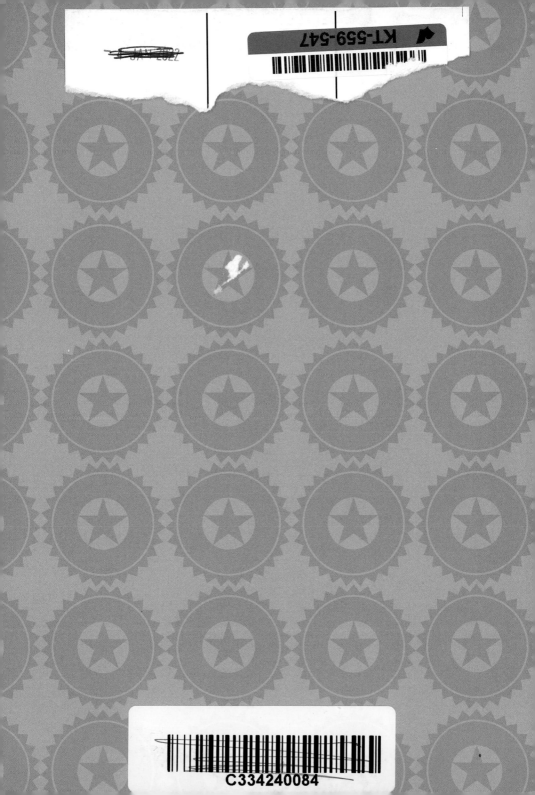

Who Will Be King?

by Katie Dale and Letitzia Rizzo

FRANKLIN WATTS
LONDON•SYDNEY

Once upon a time, there lived an old king who faced a difficult problem. Who should be the next king? Usually the crown went to the king's oldest son, but his sons were triplets. They were all exactly the same age!

There was strong Edmund, clever Crispin and gentle Jack. The king thought for a while. Then he smiled. "I know," he said, "I'll set three tests to see who will make the best king."

The first test was to see who could make

Sir Gallant drop his sword.

Edmund disarmed

the knight with a single

swing of his heavy sword.

Crispin wasn't as strong,

but he was cunning.

He tripped Sir Gallant

and stole his sword.

Jack wasn't strong or cunning.

He fought bravely, but was soon knocked

right off his feet into a market stall.

"Jack will never be king!" laughed his brothers.

"I'm so sorry," Jack said to the merchant.

He dropped his sword with a clatter and began

to tidy up. "I'll pay for everything," he said.

The merchant smiled. "Thank you, Jack.

You're very kind."

In the second test, the brothers had to shoot an apple off a servant girl's head. She looked very frightened. Clever Crispin shot the apple clean off, and grinned smugly.

Edmund wasn't as skilful. His arrow whizzed past the girl's ear, making her jump.

The apple rolled off her head.

"I did it!" Edmund cheered, jumping for joy.

When it was Jack's turn, he walked over

to the girl and took the apple off her head.

His brothers laughed.

"Jack will never be king!" they said together.

"Here," Jack said, giving the girl
the apple to eat. "We shouldn't
waste food when people are hungry.
And we shouldn't put people in danger."

"Thank you, Jack," the girl's mother said.

"You are very wise."

The last test was to see who was the cleverest.

"I won the first test and you won the second,

Crispin!" Edmund cried. "After this test,

one of us two will be crowned king."

"What about me?" Jack frowned.

"You failed the first two tests," Crispin scoffed.

"You'll never be king!" Edmund sniggered.

Jack frowned, gritted his teeth,

and picked up his pen. There were all sorts

of questions. There were maths questions,

geography questions, and even one question

asking the name of the kitchen boy.

11

When all the tests were completed, the whole kingdom waited nervously for the results. "Edmund, you got twenty nine out of thirty," said the king. Edmund glanced at Crispin, nervously. Would it be enough to beat him?

Crispin crossed his fingers, hoping that he'd guessed the kitchen boy's name correctly.

"Crispin, you also got twenty nine," the king cried. Crispin and Edmund stared at each other in shock.

"It's a draw!" they gasped.

"No, it isn't," the king said. "Jack scored full marks!"

Crispin and Edmund's jaws dropped open at exactly the same time. "But the only question we didn't know was the name of the kitchen boy," they said.

"You mean Fred?" Jack grinned.

Edmund shrugged. "Who cares what
his name is – he's only the kitchen boy."

Jack frowned. "I care about everyone
in the palace. I know all their names."

"So it's a tie!" huffed Crispin, folding his arms.

"We've each won one test. What now?"

"It isn't a tie," said the king. "There is a clear winner."

"It's me!" Edmund cried, happily. "I beat Sir Gallant and knocked the apple off the girl's head!"

"But you didn't shoot it off, like I did!" Crispin argued. "And I disarmed Sir Gallant. It must be me!"

"My sons, the tests were not to prove who was best at fighting or archery, but to find out who would be the best king," their father sighed. Crispin and Edmund frowned at each other. "So who did you choose?" they asked.

The king smiled. "Jack," he replied.

Jack's brothers opened their mouths in shock.

"Jack!" they cried together.

"Me?" gasped Jack.

"It's good to have strength, skill, and knowledge," their father said. "But to be a good king, it is more important to be kind and wise, and to care about all the people in your kingdom, from the richest to the poorest."

The king looked at Jack.

"My son," he said, "you are kind, wise and caring. You will be a great king."

The king took off his crown and put it on Jack's head.

"Hooray!" cheered the crowd.

"Long live King Jack!"

Story order

Look at these 5 pictures and captions.
Put the pictures in the right order
to retell the story.

The king announces the results.

The king decides to set some tests.

3

King Jack becomes the new king.

4

The written test has lots of questions.

5

Jack loses the archery test.

Independent Reading

This series is designed to provide an opportunity for your child to read on their own. These notes are written for you to help your child choose a book and to read it independently.

In school, your child's teacher will often be using reading books which have been banded to support the process of learning to read. Use the book band colour your child is reading in school to help you make a good choice. *Who Will Be King?* is a good choice for children reading at White Band in their classroom to read independently.

The aim of independent reading is to read this book with ease, so that your child enjoys the story and relates it to their own experiences.

About the book

The King is old and must choose one of his sons to be the next king. Usually it's the eldest but his sons are triplets. So the king sets a series of tests to find out who most deserves to inherit the throne.

Before reading

Help your child to learn how to make good choices by asking: "Why did you choose this book? Why do you think you will enjoy it?" Look at the cover together and ask: What is this story going to be about? What does the clothing of the characters tell you about the story setting?" Remind your child that they can break longer words into syllables or sound out groups of letters to make a word if they get stuck.

Decide together whether your child will read the story independently or read it aloud to you.

During reading

Remind your child of what they know and what they can do independently. If reading aloud, support your child if they hesitate or ask for help by telling the word. If reading to themselves, remind your child that they can come and ask for your help if stuck.

After reading

Support comprehension by asking your child to tell you about the story. Use the story order puzzle to encourage your child to retell the story in the right sequence, in their own words. The correct sequence can be found on the next page.

Help your child think about the messages in the book that go beyond the story and ask: "What qualities did the old king look for when choosing a new king? Why? What lessons did Jack's brothers learn?"

Give your child a chance to respond to the story: "Do you think Jack deserved to win? Why? What other qualities do you think you need to be a good ruler?"

Extending learning

Help your child predict other possible endings for the story by asking: "What would happen if one of the other brothers had won all the tests? What sort of king do you think they would make? What other tests could you have to find out what someone is like?" In the classroom, your child's teacher may be teaching different kinds of sentences. There are many examples in this book that you could look at with your child, including statements, commands, exclamations and questions. Find these together and point out how the end punctuation can help us understand the meaning of the book.

Franklin Watts
First published in Great Britain in 2018
by The Watts Publishing Group

Series Editors: Jackie Hamley and Melanie Palmer
Series Advisors: Dr Sue Bodman and Glen Franklin
Series Designer: Peter Scoulding

A CIP catalogue record for this book is
available from the British Library.

ISBN 978 1 4451 6273 7 (hbk)
ISBN 978 1 4451 62751 (pbk)
ISBN 978 1 4451 6274 4 (library ebook)

Printed in China

Franklin Watts
An imprint of
Hachette Children's Group
Part of The Watts Publishing Group
Carmelite House
50 Victoria Embankment
London EC4Y 0DZ

An Hachette UK Company
www.hachette.co.uk

www.franklinwatts.co.uk

Answer to Story order: 2, 5, 4, 1, 3

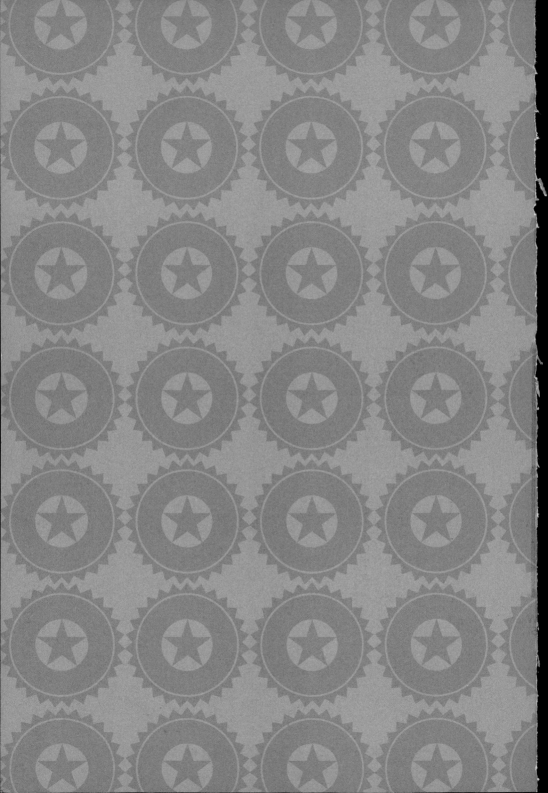